Tit for Tat

TIT FOR TAT

and other Latvian Folk Tales

Retold by Mae Durham

from the translation of Skaidrite Rubene-Koo

Notes by Alan Dundes

Illustrated by Harriet Pincus

Harcourt, Brace & World, Inc., New York

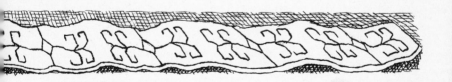

Copyright © 1967 by Mae J. Durham

First edition

Library of Congress Catalog Card Number: AC 67-10204

Printed in the United States of America

To Edwin

Contents

Tit for Tat

The Bad-Tempered Wife

There was once a man whose wife was so bad-tempered that he could not manage her, no matter how he tried. One day, in order to escape from his wife's temper, he went into the forest seeking peace of mind. As he sought peace of mind, he found something else besides, a deep, deep hole.

When he returned to his home, he said to his wife, "You cannot imagine what I have found in the forest! A deep, deep hole with a huge pot of money in it."

"Is that so?" exclaimed his wife. "And you are only telling me about it? You simpleton! Did you not have the sense to bring the money home?"

"No, my dear. I will not crawl for money. If you want the money, you shall have to crawl for it yourself."

The next morning the poor husband had less peace than he had had the day before. He could find peace nowhere, not even in a crack in the wall.

His wife demanded to be taken to the hole and the pot of money. There was nothing else to be done. Starting from the house, they soon reached the deep hole in the forest. The poor man's troubles did not end there. His wife cajoled him, demanding to know how she was to get the pot of money when the hole was so deep.

"Is it my fault that the hole is so deep?" complained the husband. "Bend over a little more; reach down a little farther. Perhaps then you can get hold of the pot."

His wife stretched and reached, reached and stretched. Suddenly, she fell over, head first into the hole. Not knowing what else to do, the man turned homeward, knowing at least that he would not be troubled by his wife for a little while. But the more he thought about it, the worse he felt. Surely there was something he could do. At last he thought of a plan. Taking a long rope, he tied a small board to the end of it. When he reached the hole, he lowered the board into the hole. Then he started to pull. He pulled and pulled and pulled with all his might. It was surprising how heavy his wife had become, but at long last he had pulled her out.

Then he looked at the board and was overcome with fright. Instead of his wife, there sat the devil himself on the board.

The devil looked at the man and said, "How good it is, brother, that you pulled me out of that hole. Why just yesterday a terribly bad-tempered woman came down into the hole, and not a moment of peace have I had since. There was no place to be safe from her biting tongue."

Without a word the husband started to push the devil back into the hole. How the devil begged the man to stop! Why he would make the man happy for the rest of his life!

"Happy for the rest of my life? First, you must tell me how you can do that."

"Well," said the devil, "take this stick that I have, go across the river, and cure the ailing baron who lives there. All you have to do is strike the baron three times with this stick, and he will be cured instantly. You will receive enough money so you can live with no cares."

This plan pleased the man well enough; so he took the stick, crossed the river, and hurried to the home of the ailing baron.

"What can a simple peasant know about such things?" the servants asked. And they refused to admit the man. But when the baron himself heard that a stranger was insisting he could help him, he demanded to see the man.

One, two, three. The man struck the baron three

times with his stick, and lo, the baron recovered immediately. With joy the baron gave the man a large sum of money and bade him go to one of his relatives, a far richer baron, who was also ill.

Away went the man to the home of the richer baron. One, two, three strikes of the stick, and that baron was cured. This time the man received twice as much money as the first baron had given him.

"Now," said the second baron, "you must go to the king himself. He, too, is ailing, and you must help him."

Away went the man to the king. One, two, and three strikes of the stick, and the king recovered completely. So great was his joy that the king gave him a vast measure of money.

The man started toward his home, carrying the heavy sack of money. On the way he met the devil, who stared with envy at the large sack of money.

"See," said the devil, "how happy and prosperous you have become with my help. Now I would like to have my stick back."

Well and good, he might have it.

But the devil was not satisfied and started to bargain.

"You could give me some of that money, too. Remember, you earned it only with my help."

The man looked at him. "How can we count the

money in the middle of the road? Come to my home tomorrow morning, and I will give you the money."

Why not? The devil agreed.

In the meantime, the man thought and planned, and planned and thought. He collected old pots, old drums, old basins. Then he invited his friends and neighbors to visit him early the next morning. When they arrived, the man asked them to play upon the pots, the drums, the basins. What a clamor there was! The earth resounded, and the din could be heard for miles around. As for the man, he went out to meet the devil. When the devil came sauntering down the road, the man took him by the hand and started to lead him toward the house. The devil stopped.

"What is that dreadful din I hear? Who is making all of that noise?"

"Oh, that din? That is only my bad-tempered wife. She got out of the hole and is so angry that there is no stopping her now."

"Is that so?" exclaimed the devil. "Then I will not enter your house. I know her well enough. She is one from whom I cannot escape, not even into a crack in the wall. Keep the money and your wife! I am going back and will never return."

With that, the devil ran down the road as fast as he could.

And so it was that the husband was able to keep all of the money and spend the rest of his life without care.

Mother Luck

There was once a mother who had two daughters, one her own, the other a stepdaughter. The step-daughter was honest and hard-working. In spite of that, she was scolded all the time and kept half starved. Her stepsister, on the other hand, was pampered and spoiled beyond any belief.

One year, and it was in the midst of winter, the mother ordered her stepdaughter to the forest to gather strawberries. She gave the girl a large basket and a loaf of bread made of sand and ashes with which she had mixed a bit of flour.

The young girl walked all day, up and down and everywhere, but could find no strawberries. Tired and discouraged, she started homeward but found she had lost her way. Not knowing what to do and with evening approaching, the poor girl sat down on a tree stump and started to cry as though she would never stop. After a while she raised her head and

17

noticed a little house close by. Slowly, she walked to the house, knocked at the door, and went in. An old, old woman rose and came to meet her.

"Please," begged the girl, "may I stay and warm myself by the fire?"

That she might do.

"But tell me," said the old woman, "where are you from and why are you in the forest with that large basket?"

"My stepmother sent me to the forest early this morning so that I might gather strawberries for her. I have looked long and hard but have found nothing. If I return to my stepmother with no strawberries, she will scold and beat me most harshly."

The old woman listened but said not a word.

The young girl felt her hunger as the warmth of the fire crept into her body. She took the bread out of her basket and, breaking it in two, gave the woman a piece. The woman put a crumb into her mouth and tasted it. She could not swallow it.

"What poor bread you have, my daughter."

"Oh, that is the kind my stepmother always gives me."

The old woman reached for a loaf of her own bread and gave it to the young girl. It was white and light and most tasteful.

"Oh, dear old mother," cried the girl, "how deli-

cious your bread is! Suchlike I have never had before in my mouth."

When she had warmed herself and was no longer hungry, the old woman said, "Dear daughter, take that broom which stands in the corner and sweep all the paths around this house. Then you will find as many strawberries as you could ever wish for."

Taking the broom, the girl went out of doors and began to sweep the paths. As she swept, she noticed, suddenly, strawberries all about her in the snow— baskets and basketsful. She filled her basket with the tender, sweet berries and ran into the house, not knowing how to thank the old woman. Bidding the woman good-by, she turned to go home. The old woman walked to the road with her, where she gave the girl a small box.

"Keep this box closed. Open it only after three days have passed. In this box you will find your luck."

But the stepdaughter wondered. "Do I have such a thing as luck?"

"Yes, yes," said the old woman, "in that box lies your luck."

"Then, perhaps, you are Mother Luck herself?"

"That I am," answered the old woman and vanished.

The young girl went home happily. She gave the strawberries to her stepmother, who wondered where the girl had found them. As she asked questions, her stepdaughter answered, and, very soon, her stepmother had heard the whole story. How the girl had searched for strawberries all day long without any luck. How she had gone into a little house to warm herself and found Mother Luck, who had given her the good white bread and even a box in which she was to find her luck.

The very next day the stepmother sent her own daughter to the forest to gather strawberries. But, to her, she gave all kinds of dainties to eat and a loaf of fine white bread. The daughter went into the forest and, very soon, found Mother Luck's little house. She went into the house in the boldest fashion, sat down on a chair, and said, "How terribly cold I am!"

Mother Luck said nothing.

The girl pulled the dainties and the white bread from her basket and, setting them on the table, started to eat, offering nothing to Mother Luck.

"Will you not share your food with me?" asked Mother Luck.

"What? Share my food with you when everyone knows that you have everything that you need, and more?" And the girl continued to eat alone.

When she had finished, she turned to Mother Luck and said, "Now, give me the strawberries!"

"Take that broom which stands in the corner,

sweep the paths around the house, and there you will find strawberries enough."

"I am not one to sweep paths," answered the girl.

So, Mother Luck took the broom that was in the corner, went out of doors, and swept the paths herself. Why, she even helped the girl gather the strawberries!

"And when are you going to give me *my* luck?" asked the girl.

Mother Luck gave the daughter a little box.

"Keep this box closed. Open it only after a year has passed. In this box you will find your luck."

The girl ran off joyfully and reached her home quite out of breath.

It so happened that on the following day the king's son came to that house, seeking a maidservant. The stepdaughter agreed to serve him. At the same time, she offered him some of the strawberries she had gathered. The king's son was much surprised. Where, in the midst of winter, had she found such tender, sweet berries? The girl told him how it had all happened. In came her stepsister, who also offered strawberries to the king's son. He tasted them. How bitter they were! He certainly could not eat them.

When the three days had passed, the time came for the stepdaughter to open the box that Mother Luck had given her. There, inside, she found jewels and rings, splendid finery, and a golden crown.

And it also happened that the king's son asked for the stepdaughter's hand in marriage, and, in due time, she became a queen.

As for her stepsister, she opened her box when the year had passed. Out of the box fire shot forth, burning down the house, the cruel mother, and the pampered daughter.

One-Eye, Two-Eyes, and
Three-Eyes

There was once a woman who was as ugly and mean as a witch. She had three daughters, One-Eye, Two-Eyes, and Three-Eyes, and one stepdaughter. Her own three daughters sat about the house doing nothing or something as they chose. It was the stepdaughter who was told to do this and to do that.

"Serve breakfast to your three weary sisters who must rest in bed!" "Take the cows to pasture, and hurry!" "Here is the flax to spin. Three pounds of it, and it must be finished today!"

The young girl labored hard each day, often wondering how she could finish all of the work. One day as she sat weeping because the work was not done, an old man passed by and asked, "Dear daughter, why do you weep so?"

"I weep because I cannot finish all of my work. I have these three pounds of flax to spin. The day is growing short, and my stepmother will beat me if I

have not done all that she told me to do."

"Do not grieve. That is nothing. Give the flax to your mother's spotted cow. She will chew the flax, and the spun, finished linen will come out from her nostrils."

No sooner said than done. In a very short time there was the flax all spun. That evening the young girl gave her stepmother the spools of linen thread, all neatly worked. The woman looked at the linen and looked at the girl. How could all this work be finished in one day!

The next day the woman sent her daughter, One-Eye, to the pasture so she might watch her stepsister and discover how all this was done. As the two sat in the meadow, the young girl began to comb One-Eye's hair and, at the same time, sang softly, "Sleep, sleep, little one eye." And there was One-Eye, fast asleep. Immediately, the flax was given to the spotted cow, and before long the flax was all neatly spun. When One-Eye awakened, her stepsister was waiting patiently, the work finished. So it was that One-Eye could tell her mother nothing that evening.

Not satisfied, the stepmother sent Two-Eyes to pasture on the following day. Certainly, Two-Eyes would be more watchful! As soon as the two girls reached the pasture, the stepsister began to comb Two-Eyes' hair, singing softly, "Sleep, sleep, little one eye, and soon the other eye will sleep, too." And there was Two-Eyes, fast asleep. Once again, the young girl gave the flax to the spotted cow, who spun the flax as quickly as she had done before. When Two-Eyes awakened, the work was finished. So it was that Two-Eyes could tell her mother nothing that evening.

The stepmother was more dissatisfied than ever and sent Three-Eyes to pasture the next day with orders to watch carefully. As the two girls sat in the meadow, the stepsister began to comb Three-Eyes' hair, singing softly, "Sleep, sleep, little one eye. Soon two and three eyes will sleep, too." And there was Three-Eyes with two eyes fast asleep. But her third eye, which was in the back of her head, never closed. So it was that she could watch and see all that her stepsister did. That evening, Three-Eyes was able to tell her mother more than One-Eye and Two-Eyes had been able to tell. When the wicked stepmother heard all that had happened, she decided to have the spotted cow slaughtered. Her stepdaughter wept and begged for the cow's life, but the cow was slaughtered. As the poor young girl sat weeping, the kind old man passed by again. He stopped and said quietly, "Look inside the cow. There you will find a pea, which you are to plant in the ground, and all will go well with you."

The young girl did as the old man told her, and from the pea there soon grew a golden apple tree bearing golden apples. All the people about marveled at this rare tree. Finally, the king's son heard about the golden tree and came to see for himself.

The stepmother was pleased to have a king's son visit her, and she asked, "Would you not like one of the golden apples?"

Indeed yes, the king's son would like one of the golden apples.

First, One-Eye was sent to pluck an apple. As she reached for one, all of the branches raised upward, and One-Eye could not touch a single apple. Then Two-Eyes was sent to try her luck. The same thing happened. As she reached for a golden apple, all of the branches moved so that not an apple could be plucked. Finally, Three-Eyes was sent to the tree, but she was no more successful than her sisters. Not one golden apple could be reached! Not knowing what else to do, One-Eye, Two-Eyes, and Three-Eyes turned to their stepsister for help.

One-Eye, Two-Eyes, and Three-Eyes

The young girl walked to the golden apple tree. As her hands reached out to the tree, the branches bowed down, and the girl could pluck as many golden apples as she chose. And that was a sight!

The king's son was so pleased with his gift and the sight of the comely girl that he seated her in his carriage, and the two rode away. The girl turned about to take a last glance at the golden apple tree. To her amazement and that of the prince, there was the tree, tinkling and gleaming, sparkling and jingling, following them to the king's castle.

So, the king's son married the lovely stepdaughter, and they lived happily ever after. As for the stepmother and her three daughters, with all of their cleverness, they could do nothing more.

The Poor Brother's Bad Luck

Once there were two brothers: one rich, the other poor. The poor one was neither a drunkard nor a spendthrift. He worked and toiled from morning until night but couldn't and couldn't get ahead. Poor he was, and poor he remained.

Because of the money the poor brother owed him, the rich brother was threatening to take away the last cow that still remained to him.

And so, one evening, there sat the poor brother sadly in his kitchen, thinking about his bad luck. All at once, behind the stove, somebody started to fiddle, and fiddled so gaily that the poor brother could not keep his feet on the ground. In no time his sorrows were forgotten, and he was jumping about as lustily as at his own wedding. So, he danced and danced. After a while he wanted to stop, so tired was he, but his feet would not stay still.

"Isn't that strange?" he said aloud. "Myself, I do

not want to dance, but my feet, they do. By the devil, what kind of fiddler are you? Come out from behind the stove!"

All right. Out came a tall, tall man, fiddling, dancing, dancing, fiddling. But the farmer grabbed hold of him.

"Stop your jumping, you madman, and tell me what sort of creature you are, a ghost or what? You devilish fiddler!"

At this, the tall one started to laugh.

"Who am I, you want to know? Why, I am your Bad Luck!"

At this, the poor brother grabbed hold of Bad Luck, pushed him into a sack, dragged him to a sand hill, and buried his Bad Luck there. From that time on, poverty and misfortune no longer visited the poor brother's house. His corn grew, even on stones, and his cattle prospered so it was a marvel to see. In a short time all his debts were paid, and he himself became a rich man.

One day the rich brother came to see him. So and so, and how came the poor brother to prosper? You see, the rich one could not bear to see the poor one getting along without trouble for once.

The poor brother told all.

"I pushed my Bad Luck into a sack and buried him in the sand hill; and from that day on, things have been going quite differently."

"Ah," the rich one said to himself, "so that is the reason." And he hurried off to the sand hill to dig up the poor brother's Bad Luck so it would befall him a second time and sink him into poverty again.

The rich brother came to the hill, and dug and dug, and found Bad Luck. The tall one got upon his feet, half asleep. Why was he being bothered?

So and so, the rich brother answered.

"I awakened you so you could go back to your friend, my poor brother. He has gotten rich while you were asleep."

At this, the tall one grew merry, threw his arms around the rich brother's neck, and started to kiss him on both cheeks.

"Thank you; thank you for awakening me. But why should I go to somebody else? It is better that I stay with you yourself and serve you alone as long as you live."

The rich brother grew frightened. What was Bad Luck saying? Was he mad? And he tried to shake himself loose from Bad Luck by force, but in vain. Bad Luck stuck fast as a thistle and would not budge a foot.

From that day on the rich brother's life started to go downhill, downhill, until in time he was poorer than the poor brother had ever been.

The Devil's Partnership

One day God was plowing new ground when the devil passed by and asked, "What are you doing?"

"Plowing new ground as you can see."

"And what, may I ask, are you going to do with the new ground?"

"Plant potatoes."

"Why don't the two of us plant together? It will be less work for you, and we can share the crop," suggested the devil.

This was agreed upon. So, God and the devil finished the plowing together, and together they planted potatoes. The young plants grew so that they were a joy to behold. Often the devil would steal off by himself to look at the growing potatoes and would rejoice over the luxuriant green stalks. One time, when God and the devil were at the potato field together, they talked about the best way to divide the crop.

"Oho!" thought the devil. "I can see the luxuriant green stalks now. What is good now will be better later." Aloud, he said, "I will take what grows above the ground, and you can take what grows below the ground."

God nodded his head. "As you like, so shall it be."

More and more often the devil visited the potato field, rejoicing each time because, for once, he was getting the better of God. There were the stalks, greener and taller than ever! Toward autumn, the devil noticed that the stalks were growing paler and paler, but he consoled himself by thinking, "This is really nothing; the stalks are merely ripening." But as the days passed by, the sight became even stranger. The stalks were drying out. At last there was almost nothing to be seen. The luxuriant green had vanished! The devil continued to wonder, "What has happened to those green stalks?" He comforted himself by thinking, "No matter. Just wait until harvest time. Then we shall see what comes of it."

Harvest time came. God took his share of the crop, that which was below the ground. And what beautiful potatoes he had! The devil? All he reaped were pale, dried-up stalks, and realizing what a bad bargain he had made, he could do nothing but gnaw at his fingers.

But the devil would not give up. He knew how to make a deal, and he would try again.

"Well," he asked, "what are we going to plant next year?"

"Wheat," God answered.

"Agreed," said the devil, "but this time you will take what grows above the ground, and I will take what grows below the ground."

God nodded his head. "As you like, so shall it be."

Together they sowed the wheat. As before, the devil would steal off to look at the growing crop. He would feel the roots carefully, but the nuisance of it! The roots were thin, so thin and so tiny. But wait until they were fully grown. He waited!

Harvest time came again, and the crop was reaped. The devil's share? Thin and tiny roots and nothing more. God's share? A splendid crop of wheat. So, from that day forward, the devil was never again God's partner.

The Silly Goose War

There was once a man whose wife was as silly as a
goose. To his great joy, one day he found a large pot
of money. In his excitement, he forgot his wife's
foolishness and hurried to show her what he had
found. Prattler and chatterer that she was, it took no
time before she mentioned the treasure to the baron
as he was passing by. And it took no time before the
baron summoned the husband to appear before him
with the pot of money.

"Nine devils," grumbled the husband when he received the baron's order, and he wondered how the
spilled milk might be poured back into the pitcher.
At last he thought of a plan.

"My dear wife," he said, "this very night there is
to be a silly goose war, and we must prepare ourselves for it."

"Silly goose war! What is that, and, mercy me,
whatever shall we do?" his wife lamented.

"Follow my words carefully and do just as I tell you. When the time comes, you must hide yourself in the potato storage pit. I will cover the pit with a skin of some kind, and your life will be saved."

"But, dear husband," exclaimed his wife, "what will happen to you?"

"Don't worry about me. I will fight with the rest," he answered.

When the time came, the man led his wife to the potato pit and helped her inside. He covered the pit with a dried skin, poured peas on it, and shooed his chickens there. The chickens began to peck and fight and eat. No war could have been noisier. But the husband did not stop there. Taking a heavy, long stick, he began to pound the sides of the house, this way and that—no matter what way, so long as there was enough noise. After a while, he stopped the noise and went to the potato pit to help his wife out.

"You can come out now. The silly goose war is over."

The next morning the man harnessed his horse and seated his wife in the front of the cart. He himself sat in the back of the cart, and off they went to the home of the baron. On the way, the husband pulled a bagel from his pocket and threw it over his wife's head into her lap. She jumped. What was that?

"Ah," exclaimed her husband, "to think that we

have lived to see the day when white bread drops from heaven!"

They drove on and very soon came to a barn at the side of the road. The man could hear a dog howling inside the barn. His wife called out, "Who is that screaming?"

"Can't you recognize the sound?" asked the husband. "Why that is the devil torturing our baron, of course."

At last they reached the home of the baron and went inside. The baron was waiting for them.

"Where is the pot of money?" he asked.

"What pot of money?" said the husband.

"Are you going to deny that you found a pot of money? Your own wife told me about your treasure."

"Well," said the man, "why not ask my wife? What do I know about what she told you!"

Turning to the wife, the baron asked, "Tell me, when did your husband find the money?"

"Let me see," said the wife, "it was about a week before the silly goose war."

"The silly goose war! When was there a war like that?"

"Oh, the night before the bagel dropped from heaven."

"What fell? When did it fall?" gasped the baron.

"Why, it was just before we heard the devil torturing you in that barn right over there," explained the wife.

"You can go to the devil yourself!" shouted the exasperated baron, and he drove the two, wife and husband, out of his house.

And so it was that the husband was able to keep for himself the large pot of money he had found.

The Three Cups of Water

Long, long ago there lived a farmer who was so miserly that he thought every mouthful of food he gave to his farmhands was too much. So, whenever they came in from the fields, the farmer would force them to drink three cups of water, thinking this would fill their stomachs and then they would need less food.

Now, one of his hands was a foxy young fellow who decided to outwit the farmer. One day, when the farmhands came in from the fields, that rascal drank his three cups of water but turned to the farmer and asked, "Would you be good enough to give me a fourth cup of water?"

"A fourth cup of water?" asked the farmer. "Whatever for?"

"Why," answered the young fellow, "the fourth cup of water will help stretch my stomach so I can eat that much more."

The farmer stopped and thought. Could this be so? Whether it was so or not, he would take no chance at having to give his hands more food. Never again did he force his farmhands to drink three cups of water before eating.

Now, I will leave it to you to decide who outwitted the other.

The Wolf and the Ram

A lamb once strayed from the flock and lost his way in the forest. He ran about bleating helplessly, not knowing which way to turn. As he ran here and ran there, he suddenly met a wolf. Seeing the lamb, the wolf opened his mouth, ready to gobble him up. The poor lamb was frightened out of his wits.

"Please don't eat me up!" he begged. "I am so small and so bony! Why not wait until I have grown? Then you will have a fatter and juicier bite."

The wolf agreed. "I will take you back to your flock, and you can grow big and fat. But you must be sure to keep your word."

The lamb promised, and the wolf led him out of the thicket back to the rest of the flock.

Time passed, and the young lamb grew into a fine ram. And it came about that the ram and the wolf met again.

"Well," asked the wolf, "are you going to keep your promise?"

"A promise is a promise," answered the ram. "But tell me, what good will it do you if you try to eat me? I will only get into your teeth. I have a better plan. Look, just over there beyond the bushes is a hill. I will climb that hill, and you will stay at the bottom with your mouth wide open. I will come down the hill as fast as the wind, straight into your mouth, down your throat, and into your stomach. That will be easier for you and for me."

The wolf agreed, and the two went past the bushes over to the hill. The ram climbed to the top while the wolf waited at the bottom. When the ram reached the peak of the hill, he called down, "Now, open your mouth as wide as you can so that I may have an easier death!"

The wolf opened his mouth so wide that it stretched from ear to ear. Down came the ram as fast as the wind and gave the wolf such a blow on his head that the wolf fell over, half dead, on the ground. The ram leaped lightly over the wolf, off through the bushes, and back to his flock.

After a long while, the wolf was able to stand up. Shaking himself, he said, "A tasty morsel it was, to be sure, but just a little too big for one mouthful!"

Tit for Tat

A beggar once went to the home of a baron seeking something to eat. Summoning his cook, the baron ordered a bowl of soup, which he gave to his visitor. The beggar emptied the bowl so quickly that the baron asked him, "Do you care for more?"

"Thank you, sir," answered the beggar, "but I have had sufficient."

Next the baron placed a slice of succulent roast on a plate and gave it to the beggar. The beggar finished that so quickly that the baron asked him, "Do you care for more?"

"Thank you, sir," answered the beggar, "but I have had sufficient. Do what you like, but I cannot have another mouthful."

The baron did not stop. He filled a bowl with a rich, sweet porridge and gave that to the beggar. Without a word the beggar finished every drop that the bowl contained.

At that, the baron cuffed the beggar's ear and shouted, "Why do you lie to me? Each time I ask if you care for more, you say that you have had sufficient. Yet you continue to eat all that I give you."

The beggar looked about. Just outside the kitchen was a box. He filled the box with stones and asked the baron, "Sir, is this box full?"

Indeed yes, it was full.

Then the beggar poured sand into the box that was filled with stones.

"Sir, is this box full?"

"Of course," said the baron. "You can see for yourself that the box is full"

The beggar reached for a pail of water and poured that into the box that was filled with stones and sand. Giving the baron a cuff on the ear, he said, "Tit for tat! Just as you were not able to tell when the box was full, neither was I able to tell when I had sufficient to eat!"

The Princess on the Glass Mountain

There was once a man who lay close to death. Calling his three sons to his side, he said, "When I am gone, I want each of you, in turn, to watch over my grave for one night lest some evil befall me. You, my eldest son, will guard the first night. You, my second son, will watch the second night. And you, my youngest, will guard the third night."

The three sons promised that their father's wishes would be followed. Soon after that, the father died. Following the custom of that countryside, the funeral was held, and friends and neighbors gathered to eat and drink and mourn.

That night was the eldest son's turn to watch over his father, but the two eldest sons had already decided to be the masters of the youngest son. He should be the fool, they thought, the one to follow their orders. And so it was.

"You will watch over our father this first night, for

I have other things to do," announced the eldest son.

And so it was.

The youngest son went in place of his eldest brother.

At midnight the father appeared.

"Is this my eldest son watching?"

"No, this is your youngest son."

"Why didn't my eldest son come?"

"He had other things to do."

"Because you have followed my words, I give you this silver whistle. When you blow upon it, a horse with a silver sheen and a silver saddle will appear. On the saddle will be handsome silver clothes."

The youngest son returned to his home in the morning. His cunning brothers asked him no questions; he said nothing. That evening the second son said, "Little fool, you will watch over our father this second night, for I have other things to do."

And so it was. The youngest son went in place of his elder brother.

At midnight the father appeared again.

"Is this my second son watching?"

"No, this is your youngest son."

"Why didn't my second son come?"

"He had other things to do."

"Because you have followed my words, I give you this time a gold whistle. When you blow upon it, a horse with a golden sheen will appear."

With these words the father disappeared.

The youngest son returned to his home the next morning. Again, his brothers asked him no questions. He, in turn, said nothing. That evening, knowing well it was his turn to watch over his father, the youngest son set forth. Considering him nothing but a fool, his brothers paid no attention to him.

At midnight the father appeared once again.

"Is this my youngest son watching?"

"Yes, this is your youngest son."

"I am pleased that you have followed my words. For that I give you a diamond whistle. When you blow upon it, a horse with a diamond sheen will appear."

And the father disappeared.

The youngest son returned to his home in the morning. As before, no questions were asked of him, and he said nothing.

Now, the king of that country was very old. He had an only daughter who was most beautiful. The princess had many suitors, but neither the king nor the princess could decide which suitor to accept, which to reject. Finally, the king contrived a plan. First, he ordered a high glass mountain to be built. He put a diamond ring on the princess's finger and seated her at the very top of the mountain. Then the king announced throughout his kingdom and the surrounding kingdoms, "He who rides up the glass mountain and removes the diamond ring from the finger of the princess shall have my daughter for his wife."

Many well-born suitors came, sons of kings they were. All tried to reach the top of the glass mountain, but that they could not do. Lesser-born suitors tried, but they, too, failed.

The two cunning brothers, hearing the king's announcement, wanted to try their luck. Watching them prepare for their ride, the youngest brother asked, "May I ride along with you?"

His brothers snorted. "How can you, a little fool, expect to be a suitor of the princess? You belong at home." And they rode off.

Soon after they left, the youngest brother went to his mother and asked, "May I go into the forest to gather some mushrooms?"

That he might do.

As soon as he reached the forest, he hung his basket on a tree and blew on his silver whistle. Immediately, there came running to him a horse with a silver sheen. On his back was a handsome suit of silver. The youngest brother quickly put on the finery, mounted the silver horse, and rode off to the glass mountain. Halfway up the glass mountain he rode, turned around, rode down the mountain, and disappeared. The people marveled! Which king's son was this?

Returning to the forest, the youngest brother released his silver horse, changed back into his old clothes, and gathered his mushrooms. He filled his basket with wormy mushrooms and went home. His mother was very angry when she saw the useless mushrooms! Just then, the older brothers reached home full of the story of the king's son who had ridden halfway up the glass mountain, turned around, and disappeared.

The next day the two brothers rode off again, laughing at their youngest brother's plea to accompany them. And again, the youngest brother with his mother's permission set off for the forest to gather more mushrooms. This time he blew on his gold whistle. Immediately, there came running to him a horse with a golden sheen, bearing a suit of gold. He put on his gold finery and rode off to the glass mountain. Without stopping he rode almost to the top, turned around, and dashed away until he was out of sight. The people were agape. How swiftly the king's son had disappeared!

Returning to the forest, the youngest brother released his golden horse, changed back into his old clothes, and gathered his mushrooms, wormy ones again. When his mother saw them, she was angrier than before. "Of what use are these to me?" she exclaimed. Just then, the older brothers reached home, eager to tell of that day's happening.

And so it was on the third day. The two older

brothers rode off, taunting their youngest brother for asking to ride along with them.

This time, when the youngest brother asked permission to gather mushrooms, his mother refused. "What? And have you bring to me old, wormy mushrooms that are of no use? Better that you stay at home." The youngest brother begged and begged, and at last he was allowed to go.

This time he blew on his diamond whistle. Immediately, there came running to him a horse with a diamond sheen, bearing a suit of diamonds. Dressing in his diamond finery, the youngest brother rode off boldly, never stopping until he reached the very top of the glass mountain. Removing the diamond ring from the finger of the princess, he galloped to the bottom and disappeared beyond the crowd of people.

Returning to the forest, he released his horse, changed into his old clothes, and gathered his wormy mushrooms. When his mother saw what he had brought to her, she could scarcely contain herself. But just in time, the two older brothers reached home

to tell of the grand son of a king who had ridden to the very top of the glass mountain and had removed the diamond ring from the finger of the princess. Who was this prince, and when would he claim the hand of the princess in marriage?

The king waited and waited, but no suitor appeared. So the king asked his subjects for their help in finding the horseman, the one who had the ring of the princess. A great search was begun, and everyone of high birth and of low birth was questioned. Then came the older brothers' turn to be questioned and searched. They did not have the ring, of course. But was there not another brother? Yes, but he was only a little fool. Where was he? And the youngest brother came forth with one finger bound in a rag. Pulling the rag from his finger, the searchers saw the diamond ring of the princess.

When the king heard the news, he was none too pleased. A son-in-law who was called a little fool? That would never do. But when the youngest brother appeared before the king with his horse with the diamond sheen and wearing his diamond clothes, the king stopped and thought. Sometimes a fool is wiser than those who call him one.

So it was that the cunning of the older brothers could not get the better of the little fool. And the marriage of the youngest brother and the princess was celebrated, and all rejoiced.

The Giant Beanstalk

There was once a woman who had two daughters, one her own, the other a stepdaughter. While she pampered her own daughter, she forced her stepdaughter to do all of the hard work about the house. Pointing to a mound of ashes one day, she said to her stepdaughter, "There are beans in those ashes. I want you to sift through and pick out all of them. And mind you, you will feel the stick if there is but one bean left in the ashes!"

The poor girl set to work. As she picked, she wept, for this was a tiring task. At last, thinking that all of the beans were out of the ashes but not knowing she had overlooked one, she went to bed. That one bean sprouted immediately and started to grow. It grew and grew without stopping. When morning came, the girl was out of her bed first in order to start the day's chores. Looking out of the window, she saw the giant beanstalk, which seemed to reach right up to heaven.

She was delighted by the beanstalk and climbed right onto it. Up and up she climbed, higher and higher, until she reached the very top of it. She looked about her to see what she could see. There were some houses, small ones, and one tumble-down hut. She entered the hut and found an old man lying there. He was very ill. As soon as he saw her, he called to the girl.

"I beg of you, please heat the bathhouse for me so that I may have a bath."

"Yes, yes, that I will do. But tell me, where is the wood for the fire?"

"There is no wood nearby, my daughter. Behind the stable you will find the bones of an old carcass. You can heat the bathhouse with them."

The girl thought to herself, "How can I heat a bathhouse with bones! I must go to the forest and find some wood. I can carry enough on my back."

When she returned with the wood, she heated the bathhouse and then went back to the ailing old man.

"Father," she said, "the bathhouse is heated, but where will I find water for your bath?"

"There is no water nearby, dear daughter. Go behind the stable, and you will see an old pig pond. You can use the water for my bath."

The girl thought to herself, "That poor old man cannot bathe in water from a pig pond! There must

be a brook in the forest where I can find some fresh,
sweet water." And off she went. She found the water,
and pail after pail she carried back until she had
enough water for the old man's bath. After heating
the water, she went to the old man.

"Father, the bathhouse and water are heated. Tell
me where I can find some young birch branches so
that you can scrub yourself clean in the bath."

"There are no young birch trees growing nearby.
Behind the stable you will find a horse's tail. That
will be good enough for me."

A horse's tail to scrub one's self with in a bath?
That would never do! The girl hurried to the forest
once again and searched until she found a grove of
young birches. She broke off some branches, tied
them together carefully, and carried them to the bathhouse.

"Father, all is ready. Come now to the bathhouse."

"Willingly and gladly would I go, but I cannot walk. Take hold of my legs and drag me to the bathhouse."

The girl stared at the old man. Drag him to the bathhouse? That would not do. Gently, she lifted him to her shoulders and carried him to his bath. The old man scrubbed himself until he was clean and refreshed. And then the girl carried him back to his hut. She made him as comfortable as she could.

"My dear daughter, your kindness has been such that I want to reward you for what you have done," said the old man. "Go to the storehouse that stands beside the stable. There you will see some chests. Take the silk kerchief that is in one of the chests. But do not take the kerchief that lies in the chest on which the orange cat sleeps."

The girl went to the storehouse. She saw the cat asleep on one chest. So, she opened another chest and found a silk kerchief. After thanking the old man, she bade him good-by, ran to the beanstalk, and climbed down. She hid the kerchief in the little storehouse that was used by the house servant. Because she was the house servant, it was hers.

The next day she went to look at her treasure. The kerchief was not to be seen! In its place was a storehouse full of riches, precious things that the girl had never before seen! When the mother discovered her stepdaughter's possessions, she was very angry. Surely, her own daughter deserved all this and even more. Her own daughter must climb up the beanstalk and see what she could do!

And so it was. The daughter climbed and climbed up the giant beanstalk until it seemed she must be reaching heaven. When she reached the top, she found what had been found before—some small houses and a tumble-down hut. Going into the hut,

she found the same ill old man.

"Daughter, be good enough to heat the bathhouse for me."

"Yes, yes, I will heat the bathhouse. But I see no firewood."

"There is no firewood nearby. Behind the stable you will find the bones of an old carcass. You can heat the bathhouse with them."

Out went the girl behind the stable and gathered the bones. With them she made a fire—though a poor one—and heated the bathhouse.

"And where is some water for your bath?"

"Water for my bath? There is none nearby. Go, instead, to the pig pond which is behind the stable. That water will do for my bath."

The girl went to the pig pond and drew that water for the old man's bath.

"And what shall I use for a brush in your bath?" she asked. "I see no birch-tree branches about."

"There are no birch trees nearby," answered the old man. "Behind the stable is a horse's tail. That can be used instead."

The girl did as she was told.

"Now," said she when the water was heated, "you can come to your bath."

"But I cannot walk," said the old man. "Take hold of my feet and drag me to the bathhouse."

The girl took hold of his feet and dragged him to the bathhouse. When he had bathed himself, she dragged him back to the hut, and he stretched out on his bed.

"Go to the storehouse," he said, "the one that stands beside the stable. There you will see some chests. Take the kerchief that is in one of the chests, but not the kerchief that is in the chest on which the orange cat sleeps."

She went to the storehouse. There she saw the chests. Opening each one, she saw a kerchief in every one. The kerchief in the chest on which the cat was sleeping was the prettiest of all. So, she chose that one. Without thanking him or bidding the old man good-by, the girl hurried to the beanstalk and climbed down as quickly as she could. When she reached home, she put the kerchief in the large storehouse that her mother alone used.

The next morning, the girl did not lie abed. She raced to the storehouse to look at her treasure. As soon as she opened the door, fire shot out and swallowed the building, girl and all.

And that was the end of that.

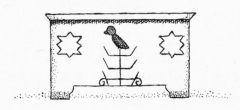

The Devil and the Pit

There was once a man who had a lazy son and a cat who was just as lazy. Which was the lazier? Well, they matched each other to the breadth of a hair. The only thing they ever did was sleep on top of the stove where the son's mother would hand them their food. That was to give them strength to lie there. The only difference between the two was that the son looked like a bean pole while the cat looked like a sausage link.

Yet, once in a while, the son managed to open his mouth to yawn or to make some remark to the cat.

One day he said to the cat, "I wonder, when I die, what reward I will have. Will someone mourn for me or not?"

"Fie, little brother," replied the cat. "If this is your question, you know nothing of the ways of the world, neither from the right side nor from the left. Who is going to mourn such a good-for-nothing as you?

Tit for Tat

Don't you know that a lazy man has the same wages as a cat? He is grabbed by the tail, thrown over the fence, and that is the end of that."

"Dear, dear, if that is so, perhaps we should stir ourselves."

The Devil and the Pit

The lazy son and the tomcat climbed down from the stove and dragged themselves to the baron's farm in search of work. But, alas, the baron had no work for them.

"Still," said he, "there is something you can do if you have enough courage. I have just built a new and beautiful home. I cannot enjoy it because the devil himself is living in it. If you can drive him out, I will give you enough to live on for the rest of your lives."

All right.

That evening, according to the plan, the lad hid himself in the garden surrounding the mansion. The cat went into the house itself. Just at midnight the devil entered the house and, seeing the cat, asked, "Why are you hanging around here?"

"Oh, I have just escaped from a horrible beast. Look! Look! There he is in the garden peering through the bushes at us. I am afraid he sees us here and will be after us. We cannot escape his clutches. Why, he will have us in shreds in no time. You have no idea how terrible he is. Please, let me hide in your iron snuffbox."

"No," said the devil. "You cannot hide there because I am going to hide in it myself."

"Then hide in it quickly," warned the cat. "We have no time."

The devil jumped into his snuffbox, and the cat—wham!—slammed the box lid shut. The two lazy ones dug a deep pit, rolled the snuffbox with the devil in it into the pit, filled the pit with earth, and that was the end of that. The devil was never seen again.

When the baron realized the devil was indeed gone, he offered the lazy son and the lazy cat enough to live on for the rest of their lives. The lazy son thought for a while and said, "Now that I have stirred myself, I would rather be your overseer than a lazy burden for the rest of my life."

So it was that the baron found himself a diligent overseer and an eager mouser.

The King on Trial

There once lived a haughty and arrogant king who flaunted his power beyond description. One day as he was standing looking out of a window of his castle, he said, "My might is such that there is nothing any-one can do against me."

Just then, a lovely bird flew toward him and perched on the window sill. So lovely was the bird that the king reached for it. It seemed tame, and the king thought he would have no trouble catching it. But just as the king's hand reached out, the bird flew off. The king hurried out of doors so he might over-take the bird. He followed the bird's path until he reached a river. The bird started to fly across the river. The king could not fly, so he must swim. Tak-ing his clothes off and leaving them on the bank, the king pursued the bird. When the bird reached the bank on the other side of the river, it flew into some bushes and disappeared from sight. So, the disappointed king turned back and swam across the river to the spot where he had left his clothes. But his clothes were not there! The king looked all about him, but nowhere were his clothes to be seen. Just then a kindly beggar happened by. Hearing the king's tale, he offered him the clothes he was wearing. The king accepted them gladly and made his way back to his castle. When he reached the castle gates, he found he could not enter. No beggars were allowed there!

"I am the king," he announced.

The servants laughed. A beggar a king? What nonsense could this be? The king insisted. So, the king's children were summoned, and the king's ministers were summoned. They all looked at the man, but none recognized the king. So, the king was turned away and had to wander as a beggar.

Before too long, the new king announced a grand ball. Everyone would be welcome; even the beggars would be given alms. The king-turned-beggar was hard pressed by hunger. Not knowing what else to do, he appeared at the castle with the hordes of beggars. And, true enough, there was a long, long table on which had been placed food of every kind. Not only were the beggars given food, but alms besides! Remembering the balls and feasts he had once given, the beggar-king began to weep. His wailing was heard by the new king, who summoned him immediately. Why should a beggar weep when there was such festivity about him? As soon as the beggar-king appeared, the new king recognized him.

"And so, oh, beggar-king, there was nothing that could be done against you? To think you were so powerful! And now, what do you think?"

The beggar-king wept sad and bitter tears. "Haughty and arrogant I was. But now I understand, and never again will I be the same."

At these words the new king took off his royal garments and presented them to the beggar-king. And, on the spot, he vanished.

The beggar-king, now recognized as the real king, ruled again from his castle. But from that day forward, he was humble and good at heart.

The Devil's Bride

A long time ago there lived on a farm a farm hand and a milkmaid. They never saw eye to eye, and they fought together like cat and dog. The people around them would watch and smile and say, "Just wait and see! You will marry in the end. Once old John and Lisel, who live on the next farmstead, were just the same. Then they could scarce wait until fall when working people have time to marry. Just at oak-cutting time, the pastor announced their marriage banns, and after three weeks the wedding was celebrated. Now they have grown children who themselves are ready for marriage. Just wait! You will marry in the end!"

Now, the farm hand was no ordinary farm hand. During the winter he served as overseer to the baron's kiln house. He had a horse of his own and money besides. When he heard his neighbors' talk, he would say, "If I take the milkmaid as my wife, may a thief steal my horse!"

And the milkmaid would say, "If I marry the farm hand, may the devil take my soul!"

But indeed! In just a short time, there they were, the farm hand and the milkmaid, married and celebrating their wedding feast.

After the wedding the bride was driven from the church to her new home. It was then that the devil appeared to claim her soul; and it was then that a thief appeared to steal the farm hand's horse. The two met behind the garden fence.

"Where are you going?" asked the devil of the thief.

"I am going to steal that horse," answered the thief. "And where are you going?" asked the thief of the devil.

"I am here to claim the soul of the milkmaid," answered the devil. "But I cannot do it alone. You must help me. When we get inside, I will crawl under the bench, and you will hide behind the stove. The bride will sit on the bench at the head of the table. I will step on her foot. Immediately, she will sneeze, and you are to say, 'The devil take the bride's soul!' After you say this three times, the bride will die, and I can claim her soul. There will be great confusion. Everyone will run about with endless lamenting. In the meantime, you can steal the horse with no trouble at all."

The devil and the thief entered the house where the devil noticed a red-berry tree switch. "Of that, I am afraid. If someone were to flail me with that switch, my bones would shatter into dust."

Once inside the house, the devil crawled under the bench, and the thief hid behind the stove. Just then the bride came into the room and sat down on the bench at the head of the table. The devil stepped on her foot; the bride sneezed so loudly that the entire room resounded. Everyone stood about as though bewitched or dumb-struck. No one had wit enough to say, "God help you!" Only the thief, from behind the stove, called out in a loud voice, "God help you!"

The devil was angry but thought, "Let him say it thus this time; it does not matter so long as the third time he says, 'The devil take the bride's soul!' That will do."

The devil stepped on the bride's foot a second time. The bride sneezed again as loudly as the first time. No one said, "God help you!"—no one but the thief who was still hiding behind the stove. "God help you!"

The devil grew so angry that he was ready to devour the thief. Still, he thought, "There is the third time." He stepped on the bride's foot for the third time. She sneezed so loudly that the entire room trembled, but the wonder of it was no one, not even a chicken, had the sense to say, "God help you!" The bride turned pale. At this, the thief put his head around the corner of the stove and exclaimed at the top of his voice, "God help you!" Immediately, the bride recovered, got up, and started to dance.

The devil turned blue with anger and shouted, "People! People! Look there is a thief behind the stove!"

And the thief called out, "People! People! The

devil is under the bride's bench!"

No one looked for the thief. All eyes turned to the bench. No one save the thief could see the devil. Suddenly, the thief remembered what the devil had said about the red-berry tree switch. The thief seized the switch and started to whip the devil. Dust flew in all directions; the devil was driven out of the door never to be seen again. Everyone surrounded the thief, asking him how he had become mixed up with the devil.

"Why, it was the doing of the farm hand and the milkmaid. Did he not say, 'If I take the milkmaid as my wife, may a thief steal my horse'? And did she not say, 'If I marry the farm hand, may the devil take my soul'?"

The young couple were happy that their quarreling had taken such a happy turn, and they gave the horse to the thief as a wedding-guest gift. They forgot that they did not see eye to eye, and they forgot to fight like cat and dog. So it was that they lived a long and contented life together.

The Guest from Heaven

Once there was a very silly woman whose husband had died. She mourned for him and wondered about him. "If only I might know how he is faring in heaven! Things are going well for us. May they go well for him, too."

One day there appeared at the farmhouse a thief, head bare and feet bare.

"Whence do you come, stranger?" the farm woman asked him.

"From heaven," was his answer.

"From heaven? Is that right?"

Yes, that was right.

"Well then, stranger, perhaps you can tell me something of my husband?"

"Yes, everything," was the thief's answer.

"Now then, how is he?"

"Poorly, poorly," the thief replied. "We are having some very cold weather in heaven. Your husband has no coat, and his clothes are in tatters. In such fashion he must shovel snow. As for money, he has almost none left."

Hearing this, the farm woman ran, head over heels, to the storehouse and returned with a new coat and a suit of clothes. She filled the thief's pockets with money and asked, "Might you take some butter, too?" Yes, that he might.

Some bread, perhaps? No, they had enough bread in heaven; only the extra things were needed.

So it was that the farm woman prepared a large pack of all the extra things her husband might want in heaven. When all was ready, she asked, "May I not accompany you part of the way?" No, that was not possible because of this reason or that reason. "Then tell me," she went on, "just how are you going to get back to heaven?"

"That is very simple," said the thief. "In the forest there is a ladder. I will climb that ladder, and when I reach the top rung, someone from heaven will lower a rope and pull me up."

The man put the pack on his back, bade the woman good-by, and went off into the forest. The farm woman was happy indeed because she knew that her husband would have all that he needed in heaven.

That noon, when her son returned from his work,

the woman told him all that had happened, from beginning to end. Now the son was a sensible man, and he realized immediately what had happened.

"You are a silly and foolish woman. Do you not realize that your visitor was nothing more than a cheat? It is impossible for anyone to return from heaven, let alone take clothes and money and butter back to heaven."

The farm woman grew frightened when she realized her foolishness. "Please," she begged, "please run and try to catch the cheat."

So, her son quickly saddled a horse and rode into the forest. The thief, wandering though the forest, heard the approaching horse. Very quickly, he hid his pack in some bushes and started on his path again. Before long the son reached the thief and said, "Good day."

"A good day indeed!" answered the thief.

"Have you seen such and such a man carrying a large pack?"

"That I have."

"In which direction did he go?"

"In that direction," and the thief pointed in a direction away from the hiding place of his pack.

The son jumped from his horse and said, "Be kind enough to watch my horse while I run into the bushes to see if I can catch that scoundrel."

"Yes, yes. Of course, I will look after your horse," answered the thief.

As soon as the son had disappeared into the bushes, the thief snatched the pack from its hiding place, leaped upon the horse, and raced away so fast that the dust of the road whirled all about him.

In the meantime, the son searched high and low for the scoundrel, but luck was not with him. Returning to the spot where he had left his horse with the stranger, he found no stranger to greet him and no horse. And the son realized that he, too, had been taken in by the thief. "I'll not stop my search until I have found my horse," he thought to himself.

He hurried back to his home, harnessed two horses, and set out once again to find the thief. But, the thief, by this time, had found his way to the city and had given the horse and pack to another thief in return for his help. He disguised himself in different clothes, filled a leather pouch with pig's blood, and bade the second thief to hide himself in the forest in such and such a place. Then the first thief set forth to find the farmer's son. Along came the son with his two horses, the dust whirling on all sides. He brought the horses to a halt when he saw the man and asked, "Have you seen such and such a man with a large pack and with such and such a horse?"

"No, that I have not seen. Tell me, what is troubling you and why are you hurrying so?"

The son told him everything.

"Now, all may yet be well," said the thief. "I happen to be a soothsayer, and I can tell you who has stolen the horse. But I cannot tell you here. We must go to a rye field, and there I can tell you. We can leave your horses here at the edge of the forest."

The son tied his horses to a tree at the edge of the forest and followed the thief to a rye field. The thief crawled into a rye stack, saying, "If blood comes out from the rye stack, you will find your horse."

The son watched the rye stack carefully. In the

meantime, the thief pierced his leather pouch with a knife, and blood spurted in all directions. The son shouted gleefully, "It is coming! Blood is coming forth!"

The thief crawled out from the rye stack, saying, "You see, because blood has come out of the rye stack, you will surely find your horse."

The two returned to the edge of the forest where the son had left his horses. They were no longer there. The second thief had stolen the two horses. The shouts and the laments of the son were pitiful, but the thief merely said, "Do not worry. The blood coming from the rye stack means that you will find your horses."

So, the two men went down the road to the city in search of the horses. It was market day, and crowds of people were all about. Both men went on and on, up and down, looking and looking. Suddenly, the thief vanished in the crowds. The son started to shout and call, "Friend! Friend! What has happened to you? Where have you disappeared?" But no trace was left of *that* friend.

Now, at last, the son realized that he had been deceived again. Sadly, he thought to himself, "Mother was silly. But look at me, her sensible son. I have been taken in not once but twice by that scoundrel. Can I be any less silly or foolish than she?"

Good Luck and Bad Luck

Good Luck and Bad Luck were standing at a cross-road at the top of a mountain. As they stood there, they saw a man who had been drinking and who was reeling his way down the road. Bad Luck said, "Do you see that man? I should like to make him happy."

"You? You should like to make him happy?" Good Luck laughed. "Why, to this moment you have never made a single soul happy. Wherever you have set your foot, you have left behind nothing but a track of unhappiness."

Bad Luck insisted, "I will make that man happy." So, she ran ahead a short way and dropped a pile of gold right in the middle of the road.

At that moment the man thought to himself, "I wonder, if I were blind, just how I would walk." No sooner thought than done. He put his hands over his eyes and, reeling and talking to himself, passed by the pile of gold.

Tit for Tat

"Do you see?" said Good Luck. "And didn't I tell you? You do not have it in your power to make a single man happy. Your pile of gold was no help at all. Now watch me. I will make that man happy with no more than three groats."

So, Good Luck ran ahead a short way and dropped the three coins right in the middle of the road. The man, having tried to walk as though he were blind, now took his hands away from his eyes and tried to walk straight, as though he had not been drinking. Seeing the three groats on the road, he exclaimed, "Look! What luck! Three whole groats. Now I can buy something for my children, and won't that make them happy!"

And, indeed, with those coins the man bought ten plums, which he tied up in his kerchief. Hanging the bundle on a stick, he put the stick over his shoulder and continued toward his home. On his way he passed the castle of the king. The king had one daughter, a princess, who had been ailing for a long time. As she sat sadly at her window, she saw the man with the bundle pass by.

"I wonder what is in that bundle," she thought. And immediately she sent a maid to find out. The maid overtook the man and stopped him. "What is it that you have in the kerchief? I will take whatever it is to the princess, who will pay you well for it."

Good Luck and Bad Luck

The man hesitated. "I have seven children at home, and I want them to have these plums." The servant insisted. So, the man gave one plum to the servant, saying, "Have it then, and take the plum to your princess. God willing, may she enjoy it."

The princess tasted and ate the plum with relish. It refreshed her spirit as no other fruit had ever refreshed her. More plums she must have; that she knew. The servant once again was sent to overtake the man. She reached him just as he was entering his home. His seven children came running to greet him. their eyes aglow. The man untied his kerchief and gave each of his seven children one plum.

The servant spoke up. "My princess desires more of your plums. She will pay you well for them."

The man looked at his children and glanced at the two remaining plums. Well, at least his children had one plum each. Turning to the servant, he gave her the two remaining plums, saying, "So take them and be gone. God willing, may the princess be helped."

The princess ate the plums immediately and found her spirit so refreshed that she recovered from her illness. She rewarded the man with money enough that he became a rich man, able to live happily with his wife and seven children in a large and beautiful home.

Good Luck and Bad Luck met once again at a crossroad at the top of a mountain. "Now, do you see," said Good Luck, "the difference between you and me? I was able to bring happiness to a man with nothing but three groats. Yet you, Bad Luck, could do nothing with a pile of gold."

The Angry Baron

On a rich estate there once lived a harsh and cruel baron. He drove and beat his peasants so, may God protect us! Once, during the holy feast days, the baron ordered the peasants to come and thresh his corn. Everyone knew that if the baron called, one must obey. There was nothing to be done about it—not even on the holy feast days. And so it was. There was the overseer, stick in hand, ordering the people about. He jeered at them, saying, "See, isn't the baron right? Never better threshing than on the holy days!"

Suddenly, whence he came, whence not, a gray-haired old man appeared at the side of the overseer. The overseer tried to drive him to work, but the old one would not work. In great anger the overseer ran to the baron, and the baron himself came over. The old man must work. The old man did not obey.

"Go, overseer," shouted the baron blue with anger, "bring the beating sticks! I shall teach him to work when I bid him to!"

Tit for Tat

The old man said, "Do not bring the beating sticks; rather bring a bridle."

The overseer brought both—the beating sticks and the bridle. Immediately, the baron seized the sticks to beat the old man, but at the same time the old one seized the bridle, threw it over the baron's head, and shouted, "Ptruu!" On the spot the baron turned into a white horse.

The old one jumped on his back, gave him a few good raps with the sticks, and rode away like the wind. He did not stop until he reached the home of a poor peasant who lived on the baron's estate.

Evening came. The old one tied the white horse at the post and asked the peasant for a night's lodging. The farmer took him in but complained. "See how the baron has utterly destroyed my household. Day and night I spend doing only the baron's work. I have not time to cut and bring in my own corn; so, see, it has sprouted in the field. Neither have I had time to cut the hay for the horses, the cows, the sheep. They have all perished from hunger. So, you see, I can neither treat a guest right and proper nor can I feed your horse."

"All right; all right. However you treat me will be right. But go at least and lead my horse into the stable. Set some straw before him if you have nothing else."

The farmer took a bit of kindling, lit it, and put it into the wind lamp. As he was about to go out to the horse, the old one asked, "Do you not have so much as a candle?"

"Indeed, I do not," answered the farmer. "How could I? He who has no sheep has no tallow. From what was I to have made candles?"

"Are you sure you do not have any? Why, I see a shelf full of candles!"

The farmer looked. The wonder of it! The old one was right. There was the shelf full of candles. He lit a candle and, still wondering, went out to tend the horse. Going into the stable, what did he see? All the stalls were full of cows. Going into the fold, there it was, full of sheep. Going into the storehouse, there were the bins, brimming with corn. The farmer stood like a doorpost in wonderment.

The old one appeared. "Why do you gape? Come, it is time for sleep."

The next morning the old one gave the white horse to the farmer, saying, "Take my horse and drive him well for a year. Turn over your fallow land; plow your fields. In a year I shall return to take him back."

And so it happened. The white horse worked as the beast he was. The farmer used him to turn over all of the fields that had lain fallow. At the end of the year, the old one returned for his horse. Jumping onto the

horse's back, he rode him like the wind back to the baron's mansion and let him loose in the garden. Whence he came, there he returned. The overseer, seeing the horse, ordered him placed in the stable.

The next morning the groom raced to the baron's wife quite out of breath. "Would you believe it? The white horse that I tied in the stable just yesterday has turned into the baron!"

The baroness ran out to look. Indeed yes, but he was so lean, nothing but bones! One could scarcely recognize him. With joy the wife began to hug and kiss the baron. The baron could only blurt out, "Kiss me if you wish, but be done with it fast and get me something to eat! A whole year I have chewed nothing but dry straw!"

The baron recovered, but he had changed. His harshness and his cruelty disappeared, for he had felt of them and now he turned his back upon them. From that day forward he lived with his peasants as well as, if not better than, a brother.

The Bird and the Man

There was once a man who thought and pondered about eternity. What would eternity be like?

"A year in itself is a long time; and when a man has lived sixty, seventy years, then his life is finished and death must come."

So thinking, he went into the forest. Hearing a bird singing, the man searched until he found the tree where the bird was perched. It was a small bird of many colors, and its melodious song was such as the man had never heard before. He listened at great length, wondering about the bird itself. Having sung, the bird took wing and flew away.

The man left the forest to return to his home. The mountains and the valleys were unchanged, but the fields, the trees, the houses were not the same. He saw nothing familiar. The people were strange, and they did not recognize him nor he them.

Bewildered, the man went to the pastor and told

him what he had seen and heard. The pastor sat and
listened and then arose. Reaching for a church regis-
ter, he opened it and read aloud. A hundred years
earlier such and such a man had gone from such and
such a farm into the forest, never to be seen again.

So it was. While the man had listened to the melodious song of a small bird of many colors, a hundred
years had passed.

Now, at last, the man understood what eternity
might be like.

The Fox and the Cock

A fox caught a cock and started down the road with him. The maidservant, seeing this, cried out, "A fox is carrying off the cock! A fox is carrying off the cock!"

The cock looked up at the fox and said, "Why not tell the maid that this is none of her business?"

This advice pleased the fox, who, in turn, blurted out, "This is none of your business!"

As the fox opened his mouth to say these words, the cock—shwirr—was away and up a tree.

Ah, well. So, the fox continued his way down the road.

The Insatiable Beggar

There was once an old beggar who went from house to house, from door to door of the rich, asking for this or that. Around his neck he always carried an old patched bag. Now and then he would be given some crusts of bread. But more often, all he received were harsh and unkind words.

One day, as he was wandering along, he started to complain and to pity himself. "I must get along with so little. Now, the rich people never have enough, even though they have money right up to their necks."

While he was walking and thinking, Mother Luck stepped to his side and said, "I have wanted to make you happy for a long time. Now hold out your sack, and I will fill it with gold. I see that your sack is old and no longer very strong. Pay attention and see that it does not burst with the weight of the gold, for if it does, the gold will fall to the ground and turn into dust."

Tit for Tat

Hearing these words, the beggar jumped about and danced with joy. At last he would have more than nothing to live on. Quickly, he pulled his bag from his neck and shook out the crusts of bread and the herring heads. That would give room for more gold.

Mother Luck began to fill the bag with gold. The gold poured forth like rain, and the sack grew heavier and heavier.

Mother Luck: "Is this not enough?"

The beggar: "Not yet, not yet."

Mother Luck: "Isn't the bag going to burst?"

The beggar: "Never fear, never fear."

Mother Luck: "Will you be able to carry such a heavy bag?"

The beggar: "Easily, easily."

Mother Luck: "By now, indeed, are you not rich enough?"

The beggar: "More, only a little more! Only a handful more!"

Mother Luck: "Do you not have enough? The bag has begun to stretch."

The beggar: "Do pour in a few more pieces."

At this moment the bag burst, and the gold scattered everywhere. The beggar looked down. The gold had turned to dust, and Mother Luck had vanished.

And there was the beggar as poor, if not poorer, than he had been before. But now he could no longer complain and pity himself, nor could he be envious of the riches of others.

Fiddler John and the Devil

Long, long ago there was a greedy baron who deceived and exploited his peasants. Through trickery he managed to take the last of their cattle, which he sold so he might gain more money. Through trickery he managed to seize their crops, leaving the peasants with little to eat. When they had nothing to eat, the baron would lend them a measure of corn with which they had to manage until the following spring. The people tried to add husks or straw to their bread; they ate the roots of the trees. But escape hunger they could not. A peasant would consider himself fortunate if he managed to survive the winter with his bare life. When autumn came, the peasant had to pay the debt ten and twenty fold.

But the more money he had, the more the baron thirsted for it; and he grew richer and richer from day to day. He ordered a vast iron storehouse to be built. It was there that he kept his money. There was so much money, it could not be counted. Instead, it was measured with winnowing sieves. Even then, it took many weeks before all of the money could be measured.

Now that the baron saw the extent of his wealth, he decided to turn from his life of sin to a more saintly one. First, he ordered a church to be built—huge and ornate, such as had not yet been seen. The interior was inlaid with gold, dazzling to the eye. Next, he ordered a coffin to be built, one in which he would be placed when he died and then buried under the altar. When the church was finished and was being blessed, the baron lay down in the coffin to see how it felt. No sooner had the lid been put on the coffin than the earth opened, and the coffin and the baron sank into the depths of the earth, neither to be seen again. Where the coffin had been, there remained a deep, narrow hole.

The baroness, young and lovely, waited for word from the baron. At last she promised to marry the man who would descend to the depths of the earth and return with news of the departed baron. Many barons came, but none had the courage to make the descent.

So it was that John, fiddler to the departed baron, stepped forward and agreed to make the journey. Preparations were made. All the rope in the country-

side was gathered and tied together, but in vain. The rope was too short. Rope was gathered together from all of the neighboring lands, still in vain. When lowered into the deep, narrow hole, the rope did not reach down far enough for Fiddler John to make the descent. Finally, the baroness ordered all of her peasants to give up the laces from their shoes. She ordered all of her plowmen to give up their whips. The shoe laces and the whips were twisted together until they formed a long rope. This rope was tied to all of the other rope and lowered into the deep, narrow hole, with Fiddler John holding fast at the very bottom, his fiddle tied around his waist. This time, he could feel that the depths of the earth were not far away. Pulling out his knife, he cut the rope just above his head.

Down, down he fell into a vast, deep cave. Feeling his way along the walls, he found a large iron door that he tried to open. He pushed for an entire day until, at last, creaking and groaning, the door opened. Fiddler John found himself in a large room full of steam and blue smoke. In the center of the room, there was a trough filled with glowing coals. A white horse was tied to the trough, and he was eating the glowing coals by the mouthful, so hungry was he. Upon seeing Fiddler John, the horse turned his head and said, "John, whence have you come? I am your former baron, and this is hell. The devils have bewitched me and spend their time torturing me. When the devils with the six heads and the devils with the twelve heads return, they will surely tear you into shreds!"

Fiddler John looked, said nothing, and went on. He entered another room. This room was covered with gold and precious stones. John sat down on a golden chair, untied his fiddle, and started to play. At the sound of the music, the devils came running home—some with three, some with six, some with nine, and some with twelve heads. They listened eagerly to the music. The chief of the devils seemed pleased and sent his servants to summon the witches. The witches arrived, each as beautiful as the sun, dressed in silks, wearing golden shoes with diamond heels. They seemed human, but their eyes—their eyes were of fire, nothing but fire!

The devils donned long black coats with golden hems and shining boots with high pointed heels. Each devil pinned on a diamond star. Then the dancing began!

What a sight that was! The witches seemed to fly through the air, and when their feet touched the ground, it was as if lightning had touched the ground. Fiddler John stayed with his fiddling, playing fast and faster, always faster until—*strink—strunk*—two strings of the fiddle snapped and broke. John con-

tinued his mad fiddling, and the devils and witches continued their mad dancing until John's head was whirling with the wildness of it all. Not knowing what else to do, John pulled at the strings of his fiddle as hard as he could, and the entire underworld shuddered. The devils fell to the ground in a heap, and, at that moment, the remaining strings of the fiddle broke. The chief of the devils arose, shook himself, and said, "Listen, John, that last pull at the strings was too strong. All of the strings are broken now. What shall I do without music?"

John answered, "There is no harm done. Let me have a measure of money, and let me return to the upper world. There I can buy another fiddle."

The devil thought and then agreed. "I will give you five measures of money with which to buy another fiddle. But I will accompany you so you will not forget to return to us."

John and his companion left the underworld. They

walked and walked—perhaps it was a whole year—but always they walked under the earth. The devil carried the sacks of money, and Fiddler John walked behind whistling as he went. At last they came to a river, which they started to swim across. They swam and swam—perhaps it was a whole year—until they came to the upper world in the faraway regions of Lithuania.

Before long they came to a village. Fiddler John went into a house to ask for a night's lodging. The devil, of course, could not ask because he could not be seen. That evening, the woman of the house prepared a bed for John. The devil watched and asked, "John, where am I going to sleep?" John pointed to the trough filled with bread dough and said, "There, and I trust you will have a marvelously soft sleep!"

The devil leaped into the trough, so that the dough whirled to all sides and around him. In the morning the maidservant went to the trough, put the sign of the cross upon the dough, and started to knead it. The devil awakened and wanted to jump out, but, alas, the sign of the cross would not allow that. Then the maidservant picked up a wooden stick and stirred the dough. Now, indeed, the devil had a difficult time. He threw himself to one side, then to another side, but he could not get out. The sign of the cross held him to the trough!

Fiddler John watched from his bed. "Wait, wait, brother; now is your chance to get away from the devil's clutches," he said to himself.

Very quickly, John got out of bed and dressed. He bought two horses and a cart from the Lithuanian farmer, loaded in the money sacks, and drove away. He had covered a good piece of the road when he heard a hissing and roaring moving swiftly through the air. It was the devil himself! The devil threw himself into the cart and gasped, "That was a tight spot you put me into! The maid kneaded me into a loaf and put me into the oven to bake. I tried to escape, but there was another sign of the cross which held me back. My coat started to burn, and I thought my end had come. It was just then I remembered that the stove had a chimney through which I might escape. I made for the chimney, turning over the chimney and the stove, but I finally got away and caught up with you! Ouf! How tired I am!"

They continued talking until they reached another village. Striding down the road was a Lithuanian peasant woman, enormously large, with sleeves rolled up. At the mere sight of her the devil started to tremble. "Who is that?"

Fiddler John started to laugh. "She is one who kneads the dough, and she is coming to knead you again. If that young maidservant could knead you as she did, can you imagine how you are going to fare with this one?"

Hearing these words, the devil leaped out of the cart, leaving Fiddler John with all of the money sacks, and screamed his way through the air, never to be seen again. Fiddler John, at last, was out from the devil's clutches! Continuing his way along the road, he reached the home of the young lovely baroness at last. As soon as she recognized Fiddler John, she threw her arms about his neck and cried, "My dear John! How long I have waited for you!"

After hearing the tale of Fiddler John's descent to the depths of the earth, what had happened there and after, the baroness proclaimed the day for their marriage. The wedding was celebrated for forty-nine days and forty-nine nights. Tables were set in the court-yard where everyone could eat and drink to his heart's content, by day or by night. When the feasting came to an end, John distributed the devil's money to the people. Now they, too, were wealthy. John lived a long life and saw his children and his children's children, and he heard all people praise the good kind baron, Fiddler John.

Good Advice

There was once a lad who could find no work to his liking. So, he set off, wandering through the world to see what he could see. And what did he see? A rich man's daughter with whom he fell in love and wanted to marry. She was willing enough, but her mother and father would not hear of such a match. But the girl had quite made up her mind; marry the lad she would, and that she did. Now, the lad had trouble anew. He had the girl he wanted, but what was he to do with a wife! He had not a crust of bread to put into his own mouth; so how was he going to feed a wife?

His wife would not despair. "Cheer up, dear husband. How can anyone starve in times like these? Certainly, it cannot happen to us!"

So, the two, husband and wife, left that city and went off to a farm, where they both found work as summer farmhands. When the day's work was ended, the wife would sit and embroider—and at last she

had finished a beautiful purse. Giving the embroidered purse to her husband, she said, "Take this purse
to the city and sell it, but make certain you take no
less than fifty pieces of gold for it." Willingly, the
man went off to the city.

Good Advice

No sooner had he reached the city gates than he met an old man.

"What is it you have there?" asked the old man.

"An embroidered purse."

"I should like to have that embroidered purse."

"I cannot give you the purse for nothing. My wife has told me to sell the purse for no less than fifty pieces of gold."

"What sense is there in listening to a wife's chatter! Money will come and money will go. I will give you instead some good advice, something which will last you all of your life."

The husband agreed to the bargain and gave the purse to the old man, whereupon the old one said, "Have courage, and jump right into everything."

When the husband returned home, he told his wife, "Money is worth nothing; it comes and it goes. I sold the purse to an old man who gave me, in return, some good advice."

The wife scolded and scolded, but there was nothing more to be done about that! So, she embroidered another purse, which she gave to her husband, saying, "Sell this purse for no less than one hundred pieces of gold."

Once again the husband set off for the city. And, once again, just as he reached the city gates, he met the old man.

"Another purse?" asked the old man.

"Another purse," answered the husband, "but this one I cannot sell for less than one hundred pieces of gold. My wife was very angry and has given me a strict order."

"What good will money do you? Give me the purse, and I will give you some more good advice. That will be of much greater value."

The husband thought and finally agreed to the bargain. When the old one got the purse, he advised,

"Where there are willows, there is water."

That evening, when the man reached his home, he said to his wife, "I sold the purse, but not for one hundred pieces of gold. Money is of no use, anyway. I traded the purse for a most useful piece of advice."

This time his wife became angrier, and she scolded and scolded and scolded. "What are you going to do with all of this advice? Have you gone mad? We have scarcely a crust of bread left, and here you are handing purses to beggars!"

But, what was done was done. The wife embroidered a third purse and sent her husband off to the city to sell it. "But mind you! No less than three hundred pieces of gold are you to get for it!"

Off to the city went the husband, and all that had happened before happened again.

"Another purse?" asked the old man.

Good Advice

"Another purse," answered the husband, "but this time I will settle for nothing less than three hundred pieces of gold."

The old one said, "But money is of no use. Give me the purse, and I will give you some valuable advice."

The husband refused. The old one talked and coaxed, coaxed and talked until at last he had persuaded the husband to agree to the bargain. When the old man got the purse, he said, "When you draw it, hold back."

Though the husband did not understand the meaning of this, he went home with the advice but not a crust of bread. So angry was his wife that she left and returned to her father's home. Now that he had time and more, the husband started off once again to wander through the world. His travels took him to a large seaport, where he saw a ship close to shore. Calling out, he asked if he might go along. That he might. The captain took him aboard, and the ship sailed away.

One day a terrible storm arose. The waves lashed mercilessly against the sides of the ship until one member of the crew called out, "There is a hole in the keel, and the ship is beginning to sink!"

Everyone scurried about, and nobody knew what to do because no one had the courage to climb down and plug up the gaping hole. Suddenly, the husband remembered the old man's words, "Have courage, and jump right in." Down went the man and did not come up until the work was done. So pleased was the captain that he gave the husband a whole barrel of gold pieces. The ship sailed on and on until it reached a city.

This was a city of great riches, treasures, and splendor. All that anyone might want was there, except water. And of that, there was none. The people were but half alive, so thirsty were they. Now the king had sent out a proclamation. "To him who can provide water, I will give half of my kingdom, or all of the money that can be found in the kingdom."

Well-diggers came, all kinds of them. They came and tried, but no water could be found. The husband remembered the advice of the old man. "Where there are willows, there is water." He presented himself to the king as a well-digger. So far, so good. The king and his subjects welcomed the man, hoping that he could help them find water. Off he went and—not too far from the castle it was—there were some willows growing. He started to dig. He dug up one shovelful of earth, then two and three. When he thrust his shovel into the earth for the fourth time, water began to seep through. The deeper he dug, the more water he found. Soon there was water enough and more for the entire city.

Great was the joy of the king and his subjects. And great was the joy of the husband when he chose all of the money that could be found in the kingdom. He ordered some ships and filled them with his riches. Then he sailed away, never stopping, until he reached the city where his wife was living.

By now, years had passed, almost sixteen. As the husband drew closer to the city, he began to wonder. What had happened to his wife? He longed for her. But, had she thought him dead and taken another husband? His fears grew.

Reaching the city, he hurried from his ship to his wife. And what did he see? His wife was sitting at the table with the head of a young man in her lap. She was stroking and combing his hair. In jealous anger at finding her thus, the husband drew his sword and was ready to thrust when he remembered the last advice of the old man. "When you draw it, hold back."

Just then, his wife looked up and recognized her husband. "Husband, husband, do not slay your wife and son!" she cried.

The mist of jealousy lifted from the husband's eyes. He embraced his wife and his son, whom he had never seen, and told them of the glorious fruits the old man's advice had borne, for the good of them all.

Notes

Notes

Spurred by the Grimm Brothers' collection of German folk tales in the first decades of the nineteenth century, other folklorists began gathering old tales. It soon became apparent that many of these stories were popular in more than one place. Further study through the years has shown that while each country may have its own traditional stories, these stories are often related to those in other countries.

In 1910, the Finnish folklorist, Antti Aarne, compiled an index of folk tales based on the standard collections from northwestern Europe. Each traditional tale was given a specific number, a tale type number, after which a brief synopsis of the story appeared. Stith Thompson, the American folklorist, revised Aarne's index in 1928 and 1961. In each revision more tale types were added from other parts of the world, and more parallels and references to each tale were included. The Aarne-Thompson index makes it possible to identify a traditional folk tale from a European country within moments and to learn approximately how widespread the tale is.

The particular versions of the international tales can tell the reader something about the countries in which they are found. Each country, and each storyteller within a country, may change a folk tale to suit certain needs or situations, thus reflecting local conditions and attitudes.

If we did not know that Latvians had suffered under serfdom and were forced to work for the German barons who occupied their country, we would learn this in part by reading Latvian folk tales. We also learn of the Latvians' attitude toward fate, good luck, and bad luck.

The tales in this Latvian collection have passed the test of time. They have been enjoyed by Latvians for centuries just as other people have enjoyed their own stories for the same length of time. They will continue to be enjoyed as long as storytellers have voices and children have ears to listen.

THE BAD-TEMPERED WIFE is a version of tale type 1164, "The Evil Woman Thrown into the Pit." The theme of a nagging wife who outwits the devil is also found in ballad form. "The Farmer's Curst Wife" (Number 278 in the famous Francis James Child anthology, *The English and Scottish Popular Ballads*) tells much the same story in song. Notice the unusual second part of the story. The peasant "cures" the baron by beating him with a stick. What an extraordinary world in which a peasant can beat a baron and receive payment for it!

MOTHER LUCK is a version of tale type 480, "The Spinning Women by the Spring," one of the most popular tales in the world. There are well-known versions of it throughout Europe and in southern Asia and Japan. Professor Warren Roberts of Indiana University has written a book on tale type 480, "The Tale of the Kind and the Unkind Girls" (Berlin, 1958). After reading one thousand versions, he was able to distinguish special forms of the tale. For example, in southern Europe and the Near East, the heroine, mistreated by her wicked stepmother, is sent to the river to wash the intestines of helpful but slain animals. The river carries them off, and the heroine follows them until she comes to the house of three old women or fairies. She does the household chores asked of her and is rewarded by having a golden star placed on her forehead. The ugly stepsister tries to do the same thing, but she refuses to do the chores. She is punished by having a donkey's tail placed on her forehead. Another principal form of the tale with more than four hundred versions, more popular in northern Europe, tells of the girl who meets a cow or apple tree on the way to the house of the old woman. At the old woman's house the girl chooses the plainer box. Returning to her home, she opens the box and finds gold. The stepsister, in her turn, receives a box of snakes or fire. The search for strawberries in the snow marks a special group of versions of this tale type.

ONE-EYE, TWO-EYES, AND THREE-EYES is a standard European tale, type 511, and is related in some ways to Cinderella (tale type 510A).

THE POOR BROTHER'S BAD LUCK, a fairly common European tale, is a version of tale type 735A. The theme of an envious, greedy brother or sister who tries to take something from a poor relative or to duplicate a poor relative's finding a fortune is very common in Latvian folklore. In the world of the folk tale, the rich become poor, and the poor become rich. One can see how this story would appeal to poor peasants who worked long hours for rich landowners.

THE DEVIL'S PARTNERSHIP is a version of tale type 1030, "The Crop Division." In this very popular European tale, the characters are usually either animals, or a man and an ogre. The fact that the characters in this Latvian version are God and the devil suggests the importance of religion in Latvia. Remembering that the Latvian peasant worked for the land barons and received very little in return, this tale of unequal distribution of crops is important to a poor Latvian. This is probably why the baron is often associated with or sent to the devil. Naturally, the peasant would rather be associated with God.

THE SILLY GOOSE WAR is a beautiful version of tale type 1381, "The Talkative Wife and the Discovered Treasure." This European tale is popular in Finland, Estonia, and Lithuania. In some versions, the husband puts a bird in a fish net and a fish in a bird trap. There are many other tales in which a fool's words are disproved in similar ways. In a Turkish tale, the mother of a foolish boy who has killed a man convinces her son that it has rained sausages. Later, when the boy says that he killed the man on the night it rained sausages, no one believes him.

THE THREE CUPS OF WATER is one of a cycle of stories about a master or farmer and a servant. This cycle, popular in Scandinavia and northern Europe generally, tells of a stingy farmer who gives very little food and money to his hired help. The clever servant, usually through some kind of trickery, forces the farmer to be fair. Under the general tale type 1567, "Hungry Servant Reproaches Stingy Master," there is a tale reported in Finland and Estonia, type 1567A, "Stingy Innkeeper Cured of Serving Weak Beer." In this tale, the innkeeper always gave the servants a pitcher of weak beer before their meals in order to fill their stomachs. One servant claimed that the beer helped clear his stomach so he would be able to eat more. The innkeeper stopped serving the beer.

THE WOLF AND THE RAM is an example of tale type 122, "The Wolf Loses His Prey." The false plea of the prey may be to allow him to catch a more desirable victim for the wolf (122D), or he may urge the wolf to wait for a fatter relative (122E) as in "The Three Billy Goats Gruff." The "wait till I am fat enough" trick (122F) is more common than ramming the wolf (122M*), which is apparently a Latvian invention.

TIT FOR TAT seems to be in the master-servant cycle style because the beggar-trickster is able to turn the table on the baron. The exchange of blows reminds us of tale type 1557, "Box on the Ear Returned," a tale found in Finland, Sweden, Lithuania, and Russia among other countries.

THE PRINCESS ON THE GLASS MOUNTAIN is a fine version of tale type 530, "The Princess on the Glass Mountain." This is one of the most popular folk tales in northern Europe.

THE GIANT BEANSTALK is another version of tale type 480. See notes for MOTHER LUCK. This Latvian version with the "heating the bath" theme has been reported only from Sweden, Finland, Estonia, and Russia.

THE DEVIL AND THE PIT seems to be a version of 1167*, "The Youth Imprisons the Devil in His Own Iron House," a tale from Lapland. The characters of a boy and a cat, however, suggest that this Latvian tale may relate to type 545, "The Cat as Helper." In this type, of which "Puss in Boots" is an example, the cat usually tricks the giant into becoming a mouse rather than entering a snuffbox. Substituting the devil, a popular character in Latvian folk tales and legends, for a giant or ogre is not uncommon in folk tales.

THE KING ON TRIAL is a version of tale type 757, "The King's Haughtiness Punished." In many versions, God sends an angel to take the king's place until he repents. This tale is found in countries as different as Iceland and China.

THE DEVIL'S BRIDE is a version of tale type 813, "A Careless Word Summons the Devil." This tale shows the power of the spoken word and the danger of taking the devil's name in vain. The repentant thief who foils the devil's attempt to obtain a soul may be a popular reflection of the Crucifixion tradition in which one of the two thieves crucified with Jesus is supposed to have repented his evil ways.

THE GUEST FROM HEAVEN is a delightful version of tale type 1540, "The Student from Paradise (Paris)." In some versions, a student tells a woman that he comes from Paris. The woman thinks he has said Paradise and gives him goods and money to take to her husband. The second part in which the woman's son is also tricked is traditional. The tale is very popular in parts of northern Europe—Finland, Sweden, Lithuania, and Ireland.

GOOD LUCK AND BAD LUCK is not a widely reported story. It may be related to tale type 946C, "Luck and Blessing Contest," a Hungarian tale in which luck fails to make a man rich with treasure but blessing succeeds with a small gift. It is related to type 947A, "Bad Luck Cannot Be Arrested," in which a rich man leaves money for a poor man who closes his eyes and fails to see it, and to type 842, "The Man Who Kicked Aside Riches." In the latter tale, reported from Finland and India, a man asks for wealth as a reward for his virtue. On the way home, the man closes his eyes so he may know how a blind man feels when walking. He stumbles against what he thinks is a stone and kicks it aside. It is a pot of gold.

THE ANGRY BARON is a version of tale type 761, "The Cruel Rich Man as the Devil's Horse." The landlord baron is forced to work in the fields and to eat food fit only for animals. Although this tale is similar to FIDDLER JOHN AND THE DEVIL (see Notes), the ending is different. In THE ANGRY BARON the hated baron is not removed; he is reformed.

THE BIRD AND THE MAN is a version of tale type 471A, "The Monk and the Bird," found in Estonia, Lithuania, Poland, and Russia, among other countries. It is similar in theme but not in detail to tale 766 in which there is a magic sleep extending over many years as in "Rip Van Winkle."

THE FOX AND THE COCK is a short but fine example of tale type 6, "Animal Captor Persuaded to Talk." This type is often found in literary fable collections, but it is also an oral tale, one handed down by word of mouth.

THE INSATIABLE BEGGAR is a moral tale about the punishment of greed. In one way, it is similar to GOOD LUCK AND BAD LUCK because happiness can come from limited luck, three groats, rather than from a whole bag of gold. Greed is often the crime of a baron, a neighbor, or a member of the family and usually brings about punishment.

FIDDLER JOHN AND THE DEVIL has a number of traditional themes—the greedy baron, his transformation to a horse. In a Lithuanian legend, a musician, playing for devils in the other world, purposely breaks his fiddle strings in order to convince the devils that he must return to earth to repair or replace the strings. What is unusual about FIDDLER JOHN AND THE DEVIL is that the baron is not reformed and Fiddler John marries the baroness.

Tit for Tat

GOOD ADVICE is an excellent version of tale type 910, "Precepts Bought or Given Prove Correct." There are many forms of this tale with different kinds of advice. "Do not act when angry" is one of the most traditional kinds of advice found in folk tales.

For further information about the tales in this collection, the reader can consult Stith Thompson's *The Folktale* (New York, Holt, Rinehart & Winston, 1951). Latvian traditions are described in the articles on Latvian folklore and mythology by Jonas Balys in Volume Two, *Funk & Wagnalls' Standard Dictionary of Folklore, Mythology, and Legend*, Maria Leach and Jerome Fried, eds. (New York, Funk & Wagnalls, 1950).

Alan Dundes
Associate Professor of Anthropology and
*   Folklore*
University of California, Berkeley
September, 1966